MUCH
ADO
about
NOTHING

FAMILIUS

FAMILIUS

Published by Familius LLC, www.familius.com
Familius books are available at special discounts for bulk purchases
for sales promotions or for family or corporate use. Special
editions, including personalized covers, excerpts of existing books,
or books with corporate logos, can be created in large quantities
for special needs. For more information, contact Premium Sales at
559-876-2170 or email specialmarkets@familius.com.

Originally published by Sweet Cherry Publishing, Ltd, 2013
Text & illustration by Macaw Books, 2013

Library of Congress Catalog-in-Publication Data
2015942870
ISBN 9781942934295

Printed in the United States of America

Edited by Michele Robbins
Cover design by David Miles

10 9 8 7 6 5 4 3 2 1

First Edition

About
SHAKESPEARE

William Shakespeare, regarded as the greatest writer in the English language, was born in Stratford-upon-Avon in Warwickshire, England (around April 23, 1564). He was the third of eight children born to John and Mary Shakespeare.

Shakespeare was a poet, playwright, and dramatist. He is often known as England's national poet and the "Bard of Avon." Thirty-eight plays, 154 sonnets, two long narrative poems, and several other poems are attributed to him. Shakespeare's plays have been translated into every major language and are performed more often than those of any other playwright.

MAIN CHARACTERS

Beatrice is witty, generous, rebellious, and good-hearted. She often uses her wit to mock people. Even though she appears tough, she is quite vulnerable. She is Hero's cousin and Leonato's niece.

Benedick is a lord and soldier from Padua. He has just returned from war. He is witty and, just like Beatrice, likes mocking people. He is willing to help others and speaks openly about injustice done to anyone.

Claudio is a young gentleman who has also returned from war. He falls in love with Hero, daughter of Leonato. However, in the play, he is easily fooled regarding Hero's disloyalty and is hasty in punishing her.

Don John is the brother of Don Pedro and the villain of the play. He plots a dark scheme to ruin the happiness of Hero and Claudio.

MUCH ADO ABOUT NOTHING

Leonato was the governor at the palace in the city of Messina. He had a daughter by the name of Hero, who lived with him, and also a niece called Beatrice. Of the two cousins,

Beatrice was the one with a lively temper, and she was always playing pranks on the more sober Hero.

One day, some old friends of Leonato were passing through the city, and they decided to pay him a visit. These men were returning to their own lands, having fought a gruesome war a short distance from Messina. The first man was Don Pedro, the Prince of Arragon; the second was Claudio, the Lord of Florence; and the third was Benedick, the Lord of Padua.

Leonato warmly welcomed them and introduced them to his now grown-up daughter and niece. Benedick, the Lord of Padua, was a lively man and was soon engaged in a discussion with his host about the just concluded war. Meanwhile,

Beatrice was getting bored. The
talk of war did not involve or
interest her. After some time,
she could not resist
saying, "I wonder
that you are still
talking, Signor
Benedick; nobody
marks you."

Benedick was very similar in character to Beatrice, but he did not think that this interruption in his conversation with Leonato was very ladylike. In the past, he and Beatrice had played pranks on each other, and every time, they had parted with a quiet murmur of displeasure. This time, Benedick was not amused by Beatrice's rude remark, and unable to hold back, he

exclaimed, "What dear lady distain! are you yet living?"

Needless to say, this brought about a huge war of words between them. The volley of insults continued until Beatrice told Benedick that she would eat all that he had killed in the

war. She went on to call him the prince's jester. It was well known to all present that Benedick had shown his valor in the just concluded war, and therefore, Beatrice's accusation did not go down very well with him. After all, what man can take calmly the insult of being called a coward?

Hero, on the other hand, did not speak much before the esteemed guests. Lord Claudio, who was at that time admiring her beauty and grace, overheard the fight between Benedick and

Beatrice. He could not help breaking into a smile and told Leonato how Beatrice and Benedick would make a perfect match. To this, Leonato remarked that in the event they were married, they would drive each other mad in a week just by talking to each other. Claudio, however, did not dismiss the idea altogether.

As Benedick and Claudio returned from

the palace, Claudio could not
stop talking about Hero's charm
and elegance, and how she had
captivated him completely.
This got Benedick thinking
that perhaps there could be a
matrimonial alliance between his
friend Claudio and the noble
Hero. Upon asking whether he
was in love with Hero, Claudio

only replied that before he had looked upon her merely as a soldier, with no leisure for loving. But now that they were in times of peace, he had softer thoughts about her.

Benedick immediately

realized that Claudio was in love
with Hero, and immediately went
to Leonato and proposed the
issue of Claudio's marriage to her.
Leonato did not seem opposed
to the idea. Hero's consent was
easily obtained, for Claudio
was truly one of the most
accomplished men the world had

ever seen. Benedick then fixed an early date for the marriage.

Soon, it was time for the wedding. Though there were only a few days left, Claudio felt that time stood still. Don Pedro, sensing his friend's anxious state of mind, decided to create

a pastime to take his mind off
his despair. He suggested that
in those few days they should
do something that would help

Benedick and Beatrice come
together and fall in love. Claudio,
who had already thought of the
matter earlier, decided to join
the prince in his scheme. When
Leonato was informed, he too
assured them of his cooperation,
and Hero also agreed, willing
to do anything for her cousin.

Finally, they drew up a plan between themselves—the men were to make Benedick believe that Beatrice was in love with him, while it was Hero's task to make sure Beatrice believed Benedick was, in turn, in love with her.

They decided to put the
plan into action at once. The
men said that they would make
the first move and went out
in search of Benedick. They
found him sitting all by himself,
reading in an arbor away from
the palace. They took up their
positions behind some trees near

the unsuspecting Benedick.
After some casual conversation,
Don Pedro started by asking
Leonato, "Now what were you

telling me—that Beatrice is actually in love with Signor Benedick?" Leonato continued with the game and explained how he had found out about her love for the Lord of Padua. Claudio also played his part by confirming the news. "Hero thinks surely, Beatrice will die: for she says, she will die if he love her not; and she will die ere she make her love known."

Making sure that Benedick could hear them, Don Pedro asked, "Shall we tell Benedick of her love?" But Claudio cut in and said, "To what end? He would torment the poor lady worse." To this, Don Pedro retorted, "If he were to play with Beatrice's heart, he should be hanged, because she is truly a noble and gentle lady."

When they finished their conversation, Don Pedro motioned

his friends to move away
and leave Benedick to think
about what they had said.

Their words had not fallen on
deaf ears, and Benedick wondered
if it could indeed be true.
He reasoned with himself that
Beatrice was truly a gentle soul,

and since Claudio had heard it from Hero, it had to be true.

While Benedick was pondering the matter, Beatrice arrived and said, "Against my will, I am sent to bid you come in to dinner." Previously, her rude statements might have offended Benedick, but this

time he calmly replied, "Fair Beatrice, I thank you for your pains." She tried to speak to him rudely again, but Benedick was sure there were traces of love veiled within her speech.

Now that the men had done their part, it was time for Hero

to convince Beatrice
that Benedick was
in love with her.
She immediately
requested the help of
her two friends, Ursula and
Margaret. To Margaret, she said,
"Go in and find Beatrice. Tell

her that Ursula and I are talking about her in the orchard." Once Margaret left, Hero turned to Ursula to complete the plan. "Whenever I mention Benedick," Hero said, "let it be your part to praise him more than man did merit. We will have to convince

Beatrice that Benedick is in love with her. Here she comes . . . Let's begin!"

They followed the same process as the men. Hero kept telling Ursula that it would be better if Beatrice never got to know about Benedick's feelings, as she would just

make fun of him. And Ursula
kept talking about Benedick's
merits, saying that he was the
finest man in the whole of
Italy. Their conversation had
the desired effect on Beatrice,
who listened breathlessly.
Finally, she told herself, "If he

loves me so, then I too will
love him. Benedick, love on!"

And so, the bitter enemies
were turned into sweet lovers.

But alas, good times do not last long. The next day was Hero's marriage to Claudio, and it turned out to be one of the darkest days in her life.

Don John, Don Pedro's brother, came to Messina that day. He was a rogue and different

from his brother
in every way. He
hated Claudio
because he was
Don Pedro's close
friend. He wanted to have the
wedding stopped by any means
necessary, and so sent his man

Borachio to court Margaret
and have her do his
bidding. That night, under
Borachio's instructions,
Margaret dressed herself in
Hero's clothes and awaited
the arrival of Claudio
while Hero was asleep.

Don John then went to
Claudio and told him how
he had seen Hero talking

to another man under the cover
of darkness. This came as a shock
to Claudio, and he took an oath
that if this were truly the case,
he would insult Hero the next
day at their wedding. Don Pedro
also decided to join Claudio if
Don John was speaking the truth.

So, when Don John brought
the angry lords near Hero's

chambers, they thought
they saw Hero speaking to
Borachio. Claudio's love was
now immediately converted to
hatred for the innocent Hero,
and he and Don Pedro decided
to go ahead and disgrace her
in the church the next day.

Finally, the day of the grand
wedding arrived, and Hero and
Claudio, with their friends,
assembled at the church before
the Holy Friar. But
before proceedings
could begin,
Claudio rebuked

Hero in the vilest way possible.
Hero and Leonato could
not believe what they were
hearing, and Hero could only
ask meekly, "Is my Lord well,
that he does speak to me so?"

Claudio told the wedding
guests there about what he had
seen the previous night. "Give

me not this rotten orange," he said. "She has not honor." Benedick could not believe

it. He knew Hero was virtuous, and he was certain that Claudio must be mistaken. But Hero could not bear the attack on

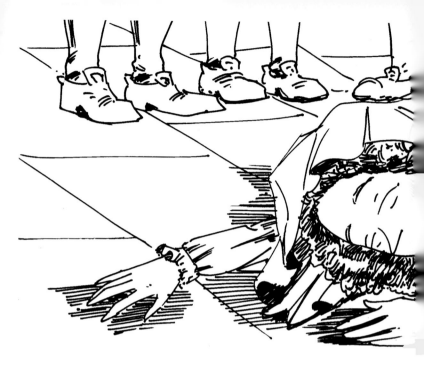

her character, and she fell to the
floor unconscious. So shocked
was she that the color drained
from her face, as if she were
dead. But Claudio and Don
Pedro simply walked off, while
Benedick stood beside poor
Hero and her distraught father.

Now the friar who was
conducting the wedding knew
from the look on Hero's face
that she had indeed
been speaking
the truth. So he
thought of a plan.
As Hero regained
consciousness,
he told Leonato

that he should spread the news that Hero had died. He even asked him to perform all burial rites for her, as then the truth about Claudio's feelings would surely come out.

Beatrice loved her cousin Hero, and knew that all that had been said about her that night was false. She therefore urged Benedick to challenge Claudio to a duel for having

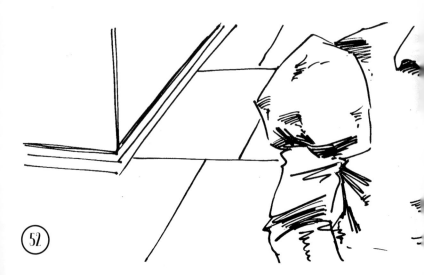

insulted her cousin. Benedick obviously did not want to draw swords against his good friend, but he could not stand to see Beatrice in such a terrible state. After much consideration, he decided to fight Claudio.

But before the two friends
could actually draw their swords,
some good news arrived. The
local magistrate had heard
Borachio bragging about how
he had succeeded in fooling
Claudio. From him, they learned
the whole story about Don John's
plans and how it had been not

Hero but her friend Margaret
at the window that night.

Claudio was very
ashamed of himself. He
rushed to the palace
to ask for Leonato's
forgiveness, for when
he learned he had
wrongly accused

Hero, his heart was broken, and he remembered her love: "Sweet Hero, now thy image doth appear in the rare semblance that I loved it first." Leonato decided to continue with the friar's plan and said, "Well, if you repent of your actions, I will ask you to marry one of

Hero's cousins. Are you willing, Claudio?"

Claudio obviously had no other option but to agree to the proposal. So it was decided that Claudio and Hero's cousin would marry the next day.

When Claudio arrived at the church, he was met by Leonato and Hero disguised under her veil. He pledged to her, "Give me your hand before this holy friar. I am your husband, if you like of me."

Hero removed her veil saying, "And when I lived, I was your other wife, and when you loved, you were my other husband."

Claudio could not believe his eyes. His beloved Hero was standing before him. It was then that Benedick told him of the plan they had made.

Claudio and Hero rejoiced in their restored love, and the friar was about to marry them

when Benedick called out to
Beatrice, "Do not you love me?"

They then discovered
not only their friend's
plot to lead
them to love,
but that they did
indeed love each

other. Though they continued
their jests, Beatrice and
Benedick determined to
marry and continue loving.

Benedick then insisted to
Leonato and the wedding guests,

"Let's have a dance ere we are married, that we may lighten our hearts. Play music!" And the wedding festivities began.

Leonato, upon seeing his daughter and niece happily married to two noble young men, could not help but declare at the very end of it all, "Yes, there was much ado about nothing. And now there is much joy."

$6.95 US
Children

Feisty Beatrice and pompous Benedick tease and torment each other to no end, but these witty opponents get a taste of their own medicine when their friends hatch a plan to bring them together. When foul play throws suspicion on Beatrice's cousin, Hero, the bickering "enemies" reveal their true feelings.

Filled with irony and Shakespeare's classic wit, *Much Ado About Nothing* is the ultimate "opposites attract" story. Set in Messina, Sicily, this play is one of Shakespeare's most popular comedies.

WILLIAM SHAKESPEARE (1564–1616)

Playwright. Poet. Actor. Producer. Legend. William Shakespeare is widely regarded as one of the greatest writers in the English language, and his work has influenced centuries of writers and thinkers. His collected works—from plays to poems—have been translated into every language and are performed to the delight of audiences the world over.

ISBN 978-1-942934-29-5

9 781942 934295

5 0 6 9 5 >

HELPING FAMILIES BE HAPPY

FAMILIUS

Visit us at www.familius.com for books, articles, and videos to help your family be happy.